Disturbance

And travellers, now, within that valley,
Through the red-litten windows see
Vast forms that move fantastically
To a discordant melody...

Edgar Allen Poe
'The Haunted Palace'

Disturbance

Supernatural stories from the Larder Collective

EDITED BY SIMON WROE

ISBN 978-1-914076-27-5 (paperback)
ISBN 978-1-914076-28-2 (ebook)

A Penhaligon Press book
Produced by Prepare to Publish

Contents

Scales

NICOLE HAZAN

It was late but I wasn't tired and so we decided to walk home past the beach. Alon wanted to take a taxi, but I was in the mood to watch the late-night runners on the promenade, see teenagers zooming past, two to a scooter, the girls locking their hands around their boyfriends' waists. It was August and half of the city had escaped to Europe or the States, so it was quieter than usual as we left the restaurant, passing old stone buildings, abandoned construction sites and fluorescent-lit kiosks where workers leaned across the counters, staring into the street. At Jaffa port, fishermen stood in a row, their lines invisible in the darkness, buckets next to them, sloshing fish. The men's clothes rippled but they were still. When I passed, I always imagined that one of them would haul his line out of the water into the air, and the hook would sink deep into my neck.

I watched the sea spraying white foam, the water slick and dark. For months, I'd been itching to swim here at night. Each morning, I woke up with the rushing sounds of waves in my head. But the jellyfish had invaded in June and I'd been busy at work, so I hadn't made it to the beach before tonight.

Alon said, 'Why are you walking so fast?'

He tried to take my hand, but I wriggled away, looked out at the water again. I could already feel the sea lapping my toes. In my twenties, after the army, I never cared if I didn't have swimwear. I'd strip to my underwear and splash around every chance I got. I couldn't look at water without feeling its pull. Alon would join me, after some persuasion, though he was paranoid about someone stealing his clothes. I had shown him how to bury his flip-flops in the sand next to a post, so he could find them again afterwards.

‘I didn’t mean another one would be a replacement. That’s not what I said.’

I was suddenly exhausted. The air felt heavy and thick, like I was breathing through a straw. Eczema itched in the crooks of my elbows and I scratched it hard.

‘Gali.’ Alon sighed. ‘I just meant that it’s been a while. That’s all. That maybe now’s a good time to try again.’

‘Like a good housewife.’

He rubbed the bridge of his nose. It wasn’t fair of me to have said that. Alon loved how ambitious I was, bragged to his parents how I had to turn down invitations to sit on panels, and charged $400 for a twenty-minute speech. I’d just wanted him to stop bringing it up. All we had done that night was talk. It was our wedding anniversary: we were supposed to go home and have sex and he had ruined it. I had even worn the blue satin dress he liked, though it was too tight, and the string of pearls his mum had given me at our henna party. Our friends joked I was the man in the relationship, the way I swore that sex fixed everything. It was true. Or had been, once. Sex was different now. I kept imagining that there was a filmy barrier between me and Alon; sometimes, when he murmured in my ear, the words became gargled and I couldn’t understand anything he said.

‘I just want to forget about it,’ I said. My dress was making my thighs rub together so it was painful to walk. ‘We go round in circles.’

‘My mum knows someone at Ichilov,’ Alon said. ‘She’s meant to be great. Very experienced. She can see us next week.’

I stared at the Tel Aviv skyline, all those hotels with their balconies jutting into the air. On our wedding anniversary last year, we had stayed at the Seascape. It was after my first miscarriage and I'd woken up before Alon, the sky lifting from grey to pink. I lay against the mattress, my body slimy and sore from sex. For a long time, I couldn't move my legs and I was convinced they had fused together. Scales gleamed on the backs of my hands. But then Alon woke and draped his arm over me, and I realised I had pins and needles in my legs, that the scales were just a trick of the light.

'Maybe I'm not meant to have children,' I said.

'Of course you are.'

'I don't want to see a doctor.'

A woman turned to look at me; I must have spoken more loudly than I'd thought. She was with her boyfriend, both spooning ice cream from cardboard cups. The woman had blistered red arms and bright strips of white where her swimwear had been. Her skin shone with oil or aloe vera that her boyfriend must have slathered on. She wore a layered green necklace that reminded me of seaweed. Her eyes met mine. Her shoulders were tense. She seemed to shrink away from her boyfriend's big hand, splayed across the burnt skin on her back.

'She specialises in recurring miscarriages,' Alon said. 'Her name's Doctor Mussaffi. It's hard to get an appointment, but she'll do us a favour.'

I turned back to him. My chest felt like it was filling with water. I scratched my arms; they were beginning to bleed but I couldn't stop. Doctor Mussaffi was probably friends with Leah, and I imagined my mother-in-law telling her about my miscarriages as she stirred sugar into her cappuccino, between conversations about Alon's sisters, both of whom had houses crawling with kids. Leah kept a rota of who she could babysit for so neither of them complained. I realised Alon must be bringing this up again because of a conversation with his mum. *Women can't wait too long*, she had actually said to me, and no doubt to Alon too. As if I had decided to lose three babies in a row, the doctor glancing at the ultrasound before shaking his head. My legs clenched in stirrups, Alon clamping my hand, the air conditioner rattling like laboured breath. Each time, I had really believed I would hear the heartbeat.

I looked out at the sea and imagined water in my ears, disappearing underneath the black surface. There was a humming sound and my legs shivered. Light flashed in the water. It could be the waves, reflecting the moon. A late-night swimmer, maybe. I searched the sea for a hand, the curve of a back. Nothing. The waves looked like oil. They rushed onto the sand, retreated.

'I think we should give her a chance. What do you think?'

There was a flash of scales, a swish of a tail. A glint of something white, like teeth. My heart stuttered. There were no sharks in this part of the Mediterranean. The stacked rows of sunbeds made blank, hard shapes. I squinted.

'What was that?' I said.

Water gushed white and spat something onto the sand. It landed with a thud. I felt a humming vibration in my sandals. Whatever it was must have been heavy to make that noise. I could see a dark shape, writhing on the beach. It made S-shaped grooves in the sand.

'Where are you going?' Alon asked.

I rushed down the steps to the beach, slipping off my sandals. I didn't bury them by a post.

'Gali?' Alon called. 'Gali?'

My feet sank into the sand as I hurried towards the water. It was like an invisible line was reeling me in. When I got close to the sea, the sand was dark and hard, packed down flat, and I could walk more easily. The air was cooler, the hot humidity of the beach gone. Close up, the fish looked more like a seal, its bulk spreading over the beach. But it had no fur: instead it glimmered with scales, each one as big as my finger. It had a long tail, forked at the end, and it thumped the sand, sending that humming vibration through my legs. Its head was turned away. The eczema on my arms stung and I opened my mouth and closed it again. My lips seemed to swell and the skin between my thighs buzzed where they had rubbed together. My heart drummed in the base of my neck.

'Don't be afraid,' I said, though I wasn't sure if I was talking to the creature, or myself.

The creature turned its head and its body flashed white in the moonlight. It wore a necklace of tangled seaweed. Its face was the same as the woman's eating ice cream on the promenade, but her body was shapeless as a seal's now, hard white scales shimmering where the aloe vera had been on her back. Her gills expanded, then collapsed again. Her mouth opened and closed uselessly. Then she wriggled off the sand, into the water, dipping her head underneath the waves. The hairs on my arms stiffened and stood up. I watched the hollows where she had rested. Alon called my name. The invisible line gave a sharp tug.

'Was that a dolphin?' Alon said.

He was out of breath. I ran my hand over my arms and the hairs slid off. I patted my face and my eyelashes fluttered onto my fingers.

'What are you doing?' he asked.

I pulled my blue dress over my head, dropped the pearls on

the sand. Alon moved towards me but I shook my head and he stopped. The eczema on my elbows glowed white. It felt rough, scaly. The rest of my skin hardened, glistening, like it was wet. My legs glued together. In the moonlight, I was almost translucent.

I opened my mouth and closed it. Opened my mouth and closed it.

'I'm not seeing a doctor,' I managed to tell him, before my throat closed up.

I shuffled into the water and the waves sloshed over my tail. When I got up to my neck, I felt my gills opening, and a relief so strong that I blinked back tears. Alon was shouting but I couldn't hear. It didn't seem important now. I tested my tail, flicking water. It was powerful, pushing me far from the shore in one stroke. The other creature reappeared beside me. In the distance, her boyfriend stood, shielding his eyes as he searched. I heard the humming of others like me, and I swam to find them.

An Unsettled House

LAURA COOPER

(Found in the private papers of the late Derek Shaw, Treasurer of the Providence Way Residents' Committee.)

> In the months since, I have considered the house number for cosmic significance, researched the architect for occult leanings, the grounds for old burials, and all the former residents for unhappy ends. I even summoned a house whisperer.
>
> Of course, the Committee has no interest in my views on what happened with number 16 - people have a remarkable ability to bury and forget. So, if only to convince myself that my interpretation is correct, I have compiled a dossier of the events between October 7th and December 21st, using my traffic diary, property listings, private conversations and group chats.

October 7th

07:00 Keith Henderson of number 12 Providence Way opens his front door, on which he has heard a knock. It's autumn crisp outside and the sun is muffled behind early morning mists which fail to lift until lunchtime. Having anticipated the newspaper boy, Keith is surprised to find a bottle of orange juice with a silver foil cap waiting on his doorstep. Across the street at numbers 17 and 18, the neighbours also open their doors, looking along the road as they bend down. 'The milkman's made a mistake,' Keith calls back into the house. Beverley answers from her seat at the breakfast table [toast, butter, summer fruits jam from a trip to Lancashire] that they don't have a milkman anymore. Or a paperboy.

No one in the cul-de-sac of Providence Way has a milkman. Or a paperboy.

No.9: Anyone missing their OJ?

Everyone got OJ, it seems. Everyone except number 16.

Number 16 – a post-war, bogus-Tudor detached residence that creaks in storms and slips its tiles - has skulked empty in the far corner of the cul-de-sac for years. The FOR SALE signs cycle through estate agents. Dressed and photographed, then stripped and left, the house sits, waiting to fulfil its purpose. People look but never buy. Ripening every summer, the tree in front drops fat dark figs onto the ground, split open like something in a Bacon painting.

No.3: Are we going to drink it?

Half the cul-de-sac drinks the orange juice, half doesn't. It tastes like childhood. Nobody dies.

October 8th

```
10:30 Post-lady in.

11:03 Post-lady out.
```

```
11:28 Woman enters - black coat, baby in
      sling.

11:56 Luke standing outside number 16.

13:45 Silver Saab circles and leaves.

14:05 DHL van in.

14:09 DHL van out.

16:56 Woman in black coat leaves.
```

October 11th

Gilman Gardner are delighted to offer an unusual development opportunity located in the peaceful and highly sought-after Providence Way. Ground floor accommodation comprises entrance hall, lounge, dining room, period kitchen, cloakroom and WC. On the first floor are four bedrooms, one ensuite, with additional bathroom. A large driveway gives ample parking and a lawned rear garden with patio is ideal for entertaining. The house benefits from gas central heating, with double-glazed doors and windows. The property will make a perfect family home. Early viewing is recommended.

October 13th

Jasper, the young springer spaniel at number 21, passes away suddenly – likely poisoned. No one is sure if he drank the orange juice, but everyone agrees that he was a very good boy. The best. There's a burial in the front garden and a small cross made of lolly sticks is erected.

October 18th

Luke at number 17 starts complaining about a noise. He says there's a hum coming from next door, and the sound of a boiler igniting late at night. Over and over and over.

Click click click –

No.17: Can anyone else hear that hum?

– whoomph.

But the mains have been off for years. Everyone knows that.

No. 13: There's always a hum.
The earth hums.
You know about the background hum, Luke?

Everyone knows that Luke is going through the wars. His partner left him and then he had the hospital stay for his neck and now he's bored on sick leave. At least, that's what he's telling everyone, but we all see the fading red line around his throat.

No.2: Of course, there's a hum.
It's probably the painkillers.
I'd be humming too.

No.23: Do you think he's got any spare?

October 21st

```
11.45 Luke and Keith standing outside
      number 16.

13:45 Woman in black coat.

14:09 Evri delivery van in.

14:11 Man in suit, silver Saab. Parked
      at 16. New estate agent?

15:25 Saab out.

16:15 Evri van out – erratic driving –
      complaint made.

17:33pm Gothic male, long coat, red hair.
```

No.2: Keep your eye out for a young man in black.
Looks like he's up to no good.

No.8: He's one of ours, Derek.

No.2: Apologies, Emily. It's difficult to keep up with your young men.

No.3: Maybe you shouldn't keep up at all, Derek.
You do you, Em.

It's Emily's youngest sister, coming home late that night from her bar job, who sees the lights. A flash of white moving between the rooms in number 16, sweeping the walls. Then a bright flash of green through the half-drawn curtains.

No.23: Could be the estate agent…

No.8: At 2am?

Click click click whooomph.

October 24th

MISSING CAT

Tilly

Grey tabby with 'V' between eyes. Last seen 23rd October chasing birds in the fig tree outside number 16. Didn't come home for dinner.

Return to No.7 Providence Way.

October 27th

01:00 Keith is seen shuffling across the green in his pyjamas, headed for number 16. Beverley intercepts him as he stands limp and somnambulant in the cold. She cradles his face between her hands before gently escorting him back home.

October 28th

Tilly is found in pieces outside number 16. The police are called, the house inspected. The estate agent in the silver Saab pulls away in a hurry to avoid questions.

No.2: There are some sick fucks about.
Keep your pets indoors.

No.3: Remember that time you found two men
shitting in your front garden, Derek?

No.2: Like I said, plenty of scum.
Police do nothing.

No.3: Can you dust for faeces?

No.2: Ha. Ha.

No.14: Lol.

October 31st

No.23: Whoever is leaving milk bottles outside my house, thanks
but no thanks.
I'm lactose intolerant.

Number 16 stays quiet. Tiny witches, vampires and Pikachus parade around Providence Way, but no one stops there to trick or treat.

November 3rd

```
11:39 Luke standing outside number 16.

13:45 Man with burgundy jumper and
      turned-up jeans, tan satchel.

15:31 Silver Saab enters. Man in suit
      again.

17:19 Keith standing outside number 16.

20:59 Silver Saab out.
```

November 5th

The air smells like wood-spice and cordite.

The orange juice appears again on a morning when the fig leaves become limp gloves in the drizzle. One leaf skitters and tumbles across the road, a severed hand waving.

'How long has that house been empty?' asks the new owner of number 19, freshly transplanted from London. 'Doesn't it bring the property prices down?'

No.14: Can whoever's burning wood stop it, please?
It's terrible for the environment and my asthma.

Number 14 appends their post with an article about particle pollution. Number 3 comments with an article about fuel poverty.

A night of bangs and pops follows, not all of them from the fireworks on the green.

Click click click whoomph.

November 9th

No.8: Is anyone else getting creeped out by number 16?

No.14: It's giving me the heebie-jeebies.
Like it's watching me, or something.

No.19: Wish they'd hurry up and sell it.

No.14: Luke was out there the other day for like an hour.
Just looking at it.
Creepy AF.

No.12: Last night I dreamed I was in the house.

November 12th

19:27 Luke stands outside number 16 and breathes deep. There's that clicking sound again and wood-smoke on the air.

No.17: There's someone in the house.
I'm going to have a look.

Thirty minutes later he sends a photo taken through the living room window. The curtains are half-drawn and the lights are on.

No.17: Can you see them?

No.12: See who?

No.17: There's a couple with a baby.
He's in red, she's in black.
They look

No.14: Look what?

No.17: Wrong.

No.9: There's no one there, Luke. It's just a room.

No.23: Luke, I'll have whatever you're having!

No.3: Lights are on but nobody's home.

No.17: They bloody well are.

No.12: Wait, I'm coming over.

Curtains part around the cul-de-sac as Keith stomps across the green and stands by the fig tree outside number 16. He walks up the driveway and down the side of the house. People start to congregate on the green. They huddle around mugs of coffee and bottles of beer in winter jackets and woollen hats. The mood is almost festive.

Beverley charges across the green and marches down the side of the house. She flushes out the two startled men, both pale and breathless as they scurry across the green with mud-slick trousers.

'There's something not right there,' says Keith, shaking his head, but he can't say what it was he saw.

Later he sends a photo of smeared colours – reds, whites and blacks.

No.3: Could be anything.

No.14: Could be two people in a room.

No.2: Could be a Francis Bacon.

Luke returns home and turns on all the lights.

November 15th

Beverley realizes something is wrong when Keith asks why he hasn't heard from his brother in so long.

'You carried his coffin,' Beverley says. 'Don't you remember? It was two years ago.'

Later, when he's been quiet too long, Beverley finds Keith staring out the window towards number 16.

'Can you hear a baby crying?' he says.

November 17th

The police are called, just to be sure no one is inside, but when they arrive the house is quiet, the lights off. Luke and Keith are cautioned for breaking and entering.

November 21st

The fig tree shivers and bobs in the winds, shaking loose the last of its leaves. Early snows from a winter storm settle across the green. Kids are dragged through the few inches of slush using dinner trays as makeshift toboggans.

Luke steps out that night to taste winter on his tongue. His body is found the next morning wedged under the sash window at the rear of number 16. His head is not.

November 22nd

07:32 Silver Saab in.

08:47 Police cars, ambulance at number 16.

11:38 Forensics Ford Transit. Crime scene tape across number 16.

11:46 Silver Saab out.

12:56 Keith walking circles on the green.

14:03 TV van in.

It makes the six o'clock news.

No.19: This is terrible for house prices.

No.23: Poor Luke. What a way to go.

No.9: Maybe it was for the best? He wasn't very happy, bless him.

No.3 Which one of you has the head?

No.2: A person has died. Not funny.

No.14: Lol.

November 30th

A lull comes over Providence Way. Talk is minimal and there are merely curt hellos in passing. Everyone keeps their pets and children inside.

It seems the house looks better than it used to, even with police tape wafting in ribbons across the driveway.

The fig tree thrusts fruit-laden branches against overcast skies.

December 12th

```
10:37 Removal company at number 16.

13:45 Woman, black coat; man, burgundy
      jumper. Leaving in a hurry.

14:13 Silver Saab. Estate agent taking
      down sign.

17:20 Young male, blond, band t-shirt.
```

No.8 He's one of ours.

December 17th

Still no head.

A new FOR SALE sign is erected by a woman driving a white Tesla.

December 20th

****Beautiful detached family home
in the █████ area****

Marsh and Knapp are delighted to offer a stunning mock-Tudor family home which has undergone recent renovation. Comprising hallway, lounge and open-plan kitchen-dining room, the property features a master bedroom with ensuite and two further bedrooms on the first floor. Conveniently located near local amenities, a primary school and motorway, this must-see property is accepting below-market offers.

December 21st

Luke's funeral is held at the local crematorium in a humanist ceremony. People talk about how good and funny he was, how much they loved him. About how no one said these things when he was alive.

Later, the committee clusters around the buffet table in the pub whispering about the house. It seems to be standing up taller, the slates in the roof replaced. People keep dreaming about being inside it, they say. Not just one person, many.

That night, they congregate on the green and watch Keith standing outside the house with a can of petrol. There's mulled wine and axes. The mood is festive.

As Keith approaches, the house switches lights on and off in warning. The crowd gasps. The fig tree bobs and creaks. No one is quite sure what happens next, but the video footage shows Keith raise his hand grasping a lighter. He rolls the flint under his thumb, one, two times. He fumbles the flame into the petrol on the third.

Click click click whoomph.

The Manhattan Beekeeper

JAMIE BOLT

Miss Bute often says at her parties that she has more than enough antibodies circulating in her blood, plenty to tackle the venom of any killer bee swarm. It's rare for the Africanized honeybee to reach New York, anyway. There's the odd case of an infant crushing one with its chubby hand – a red welt, tears, shrieking – nothing more. *My honeybees would not harm a fly*, she says: this being a favourite witticism at the parties she holds in her 33rd floor apartment, just as she does today.

A boy wearing a suit and bowtie and his sister in a yellow party frock gaze on as Miss Bute withdraws a honey frame from the hive. It is August and there is no shade on the bare concrete roof terrace. The wind is relentless.

'But there can't be any flowers for a mile around,' says George.

'Why don't you grow some here?' asks Flora.

'With a name like Flora, you should know better,' says Miss Bute.

The children laugh.

Daphne Phillips comes out from the party in the kitchen and onto the terrace. 'Children?'

'Miss Bute was going to let us taste the honey, mother.'

'And get stung how many times I can't imagine.'

'Anaphylactic shock,' says Miss Bute.

'What on earth is that?'

'Well, George, it's–'

'Shock. That's what it is. It's shock,' says Daphne. 'Come away from those hives, now.'

'Your mother's right. We don't want you swelling up like a white balloon.'

'And bursting,' adds Flora.

Miss Alice Bute watches as her closest friend Daphne hurries her children away and back inside. She closes her eyes, turns her face to the sun and squeezes the trigger of her beehive smoker three times. Through the faint noise of traffic, she can hear the song of the bees. Twenty-thousand voices or more from inside each of the five hives. The song gives flight to distant memories: her father on the farm, flies gathering on the horses he breaks in; slumped drunk on the sofa with his shotgun. Alice pictures a plague of bees blackening the prairie sky, wheeling about to settle on the homestead.

'C'mon,' says Officer Bill Phillips, as he comes outside from her party, 'Topple over the edge Miss Bute, and you're dead meat.'

'That's not going to happen, I mean, who would look after my bees?'

'Daphne's always mooching about. She's got time on her hands.'

'George? Flora?' says Miss Bute.

'Huh. I need to knock those two into shape.' Bill Phillips bats away a bee. 'What is it with these goddamn bugs?'

'They get scared. You get scared. Even tough police officers get scared.'

'Since when?'

'You'd shoot a person, wouldn't you.'

'Anyone, if they crossed the line,' he shrugs.

'Kill some kid just for doing something crazy?'

'Brute force. That's the only way.'

When he and the other guests have gone, Miss Bute bends down to the bathroom tap and drinks from it. Looking into the mirror she sees that her heavy make-up has run. Her lipstick appears clownish, her mascara is smeared. No wonder those people were staring as they left, laughing in the corridor, sharing a joke. Seventy-eight is a bad age, she says to herself, looking upwards to put in her contact lenses. Someone rings the door-bell. Alice tightens a yellow towel around her and goes out into the hall. She peers through the spyhole and sees Officer Phillips looking past her, into her apartment.

'Don't start, I just left my cap,' he says, barging in.

'Is that how you talk to Daphne?'

'I talk to my woman how I want,' he says.

'I know what you are. An abuser.'

'Oh, yeah?'

Bill Phillips pushes past, catching her by surprise, and, forgetting to close the front door, she follows him towards the roof terrace. Clouds have gathered and it has started to rain. He grabs his uniform cap from a table in the corner. A worker bee on the shiny visor of the hat stings him as he puts it on. He curses and squeezes his hand.

Miss Bute wanders out with an umbrella she keeps on a hook by the terrace door.

'What's the matter with you?' he says, clutching his hand. 'A woman like you should be playing cards in some home, or spending time with their grand-children, if they had any, not obsessing over insects. Get a life.'

Miss Bute closes her umbrella, points it at a hive and hisses strange words.

A clump of bees spills out onto the concrete. Some part from the clump, more crawl out and take flight. More burst out from the hives, and soon the terrace is alive with stinging insects. Five trails of twenty-thousand or so bees surge up into the rainy smog above Manhattan.

Bill Phillips runs, slipping on the wet tiles, but she calls after him.

'Don't go all cowardly on me, Officer Phillips. Be a man.'

He sees the scene behind him reflected in her wall panels. In the heavy light, there is a black spot which grows in size. He turns to see the mass fly toward him. It circles and closes in like a humming twister. He drops to his knees and falls forwards, landing face down.

Looking at him, Miss Bute sees her sixteen-year-old self being attacked by worker bees in the woods near her childhood home in Wyoming. Her father is looking on.

'Papa, Papa, please, make them stop!'

'They're the ones who are scared, Ally.'

'But Papa.'

'Don't "but" me kid - just stay still.'

Just like her father had in the woods, Alice now sits down by the lifeless body as the bees lose interest.

Miss Alice Bute gets up and drifts toward the edge of the terrace where she looks out over the railing and down to Park Avenue. Yellow taxi cabs queue as the rain stops. Workers emerge onto the pavement. Above, the pacifying smoke of cloud drifts through skyscrapers.

'Bill?' Daphne Phillips calls up through the open door. She approaches, screams and runs to her husband. She kneels and begins slapping his face trying to bring him round, but in vain. 'He needs an ambulance!' she shouts. 'He needs an ambulance. How could you let this happen, Alice? What in God's name have you done?'

'Daphne, I've grown up in the half-light, waiting to strike. She who has her life taken, shall take another in return. Believe me, it wasn't hard watching a sadistic man die. Don't look at me like that, I knew how he treated you. Go; take George and Flora. Leave New York, and go as far away as you can from this city. Men are poison and honey – they sweeten you up and poison your soul. Remember this: I am not angry; I am justice, and if a thousand bee stings can right a wrong, then so be it.'

Miss Bute the beekeeper gazes out over Manhattan and down at the swollen body on the ground. 'You'll find no peace in Hell, Officer Phillips.'

ROB PASSMORE

Jennifer turned the faucet and looked up. Water jetted out of the shower head and onto her face.

No-one ever really begins a shower like this, she thought, by standing directly under it before turning the thing on. This is how they have a shower in the movies. Any normal person would turn a shower on and let it run for a few seconds and then test the water temperature with their hand before moving underneath the stream. But she had begun this shower like she was in a movie.

The cubicle of the shower itself was decently sized and clean enough without conveying the sense that this was an executive hotel room. No, whatever pretentions of luxury this accommodation possessed they belonged to a faded past. What might have once been considered an exclusive locale was now somewhere off the beaten track, and a faint smell of staleness betrayed her room's lack of use. Culzean's grand and storied history meant little now, she knew, but it had another reputation.

Through the glass partition of the shower and the open bathroom door she could see the rest of the room. The bed with her discarded clothes on top of it, a small desk against the wall with the curtains pulled across the window above, as well as that distinctive wallpaper. The design on the wallpaper was of elaborate and stylised flowers in repetition, blooming effusively in oranges and reds from a web of dark green foliage. The petals lush and glossy and scarlet. The raised stigma inviting pollination. The wallpaper was clearly intended to convey a sense of ornate regency splendour, Jennifer thought, but whilst that effect may have once been achieved, it has not been sustained.

Despite the fact that the wallpaper had seen better days,

Jennifer found the design hypnotic. She looked to the central pistil of each of the orange flower heads as they repeated across the wall, counting them off in her mind.

Then, in one of the blooms at the edge of her vision, she thought she saw a flicker of movement. She fixed her gaze on that flower but, as the steam on the shower door gradually obscured her view, the dark centre remained still.

Am I scared? Jennifer asked herself.

She felt an itch on her right hand and scratched it with her left. When she looked down she saw that it was not an itch but a small cut to the side of her right forefinger, caused by an earlier slip with a cheese slice. Blood leaked out of the wound she'd opened and dripped from her finger nails a diluted burgundy. She watched it fall onto the white porcelain by her toes. She took the finger in her left hand and squeezed. The blood flow increased for a few seconds and then dwindled. She put the finger in her mouth and gently sucked. She looked up at the shower head and the rhythm of the water on her face felt calming. She closed her eyes and ran the fingers of her left hand through her matted wet hair.

Her mind drifted back to the conversation with Sally.

'Why are you going to Culzean? It's a terrible place.'

'I'm going there for science, Sally.'

'You're not going for science, you're going for a cheap thrill.'

'You are so crude. I've calculated exactly when ****** comes. There is a pattern.'

'Don't say that name.'

'****** is benign, if it's anything at all. I'll say that name as much as I like, because to investigate ******, is to advance science.'

'If it's so benign, *Jennifer*, then what happened to –'

Something made a noise and Jennifer opened her eyes. The glass screen was completely steamed up now. She removed the finger from her mouth and checked it. The bleeding had stopped.

The shower was hot and the steam made her feel light-headed. She looked up into the shower head again and let the water flush the skin on her face and she stood like that for several minutes and let the warmth of it fill her up. Then, slowly, she took tiny steps backwards, so that the water traced a line over her open mouth and down her throat and on to the base of her sternum. She stopped there and ran her hands through her hair, her skin tingling under the beat of the water. She could see tiny droplets formed from steam, clinging to the other side of the glass, amassed there and swelling.

She thought about the orange and red flowers of the wallpaper. She imagined its texture.

Without moving her feet, she looked to her right and reached to pick up a single serving bottle of cobalt blue shower gel. She saw stars in her eyes when she moved her head back from that craned position and when she looked at the glass screen there seemed to be fluid shapes moving in the monochrome of the steam. She took the laver to her body and drew the bubbles down her torso. The delicate touch of her fingers like insects on her skin.

A low noise came from outside the shower cubicle, and she stopped.

It was a noise she could not place and immediately she wasn't sure if she had really heard anything at all. The only sound now was that of the shower and water pattering off porcelain. She looked at the steamed-up window and then back at her hands. The cut had opened again. Blood mixed with the bubbles and ran down her leg a disconcerting purple.

The noise came again. Longer this time, like a person speaking in slow motion. The source was in the room, she was sure.

Jennifer put a palm on the shower door. The touch of the glass was cold. It made her shiver. She dragged her hand down the glass to clear a line of sight into the room and she saw the open bathroom door and the room beyond and the wallpaper and the bed.

But her clothes were no longer on the bed.

She wiped more of the glass clear and stood there still and watched.

Nothing moved in the room.

She opened the glass door of the shower and cold air rushed in and tensed her skin. Steam hung in the bathroom air.

She stared through the open door to the bedroom. At the dense green and the bright unfurling lips of the flowers on the wallpaper. At the space on the bed where her clothes should be.

There was a moment of shadow, as though something had briefly obscured the light.

'Hello ******,' she said. 'I'm not scared.'

But now, she realised for the first time, she was.

Shampoo slowly dripped down her forehead and into her eyes and she blinked and tried to keep them open, but it stung and she couldn't. She pulled her head back under the water and brought her hands up to her face and tried to wipe the suds away while her eyes were closed.

Jennifer couldn't feel her fingers on her face. She felt numb.

She opened her eyes and looked up at the dim outline of

the shower head and let the water wash around her eyeballs. Then she turned back to the open door of the shower cubicle and looked out into the room again.

She waited for something to break the plane of the open door. Adrenaline spiked in her skin. She didn't blink. She tried to focus on the shape of an orange bloom in the wallpaper, her eyes dry and aching. It looked more swollen than before.

The sound of water on porcelain. Her naked skin exposed to cool air. Her fingers still numb.

She looked down to check if the blood had stopped from the cut on her finger.

But when she did, she saw that she no longer had any fingers. All ten of them were gone. And now the malformed appendages at the end of each arm were steadily dissolving. The process appeared to be taking place at a molecular level and Jennifer was momentarily fascinated as she watched the remainder of her withered right hand disintegrate. Before her eyes, skin and bone and blood all turned to ash and when she finally tried to scream there was no sound. She could no longer feel a tongue in her mouth or breath in her lungs.

She turned back to her reflection in the glass of the shower wall, but her Jenniferness was already smoothed away. She no longer recognised the faceless thing she saw there.

In her mind she screamed, ******.

Every sinew strained with her need to make a sound. Then the tension in her muscles released and the undefined mass of her body sank lower in the shower cubicle. She desperately tried to touch herself with the stumps of her arms but her flesh fell in lumps of dust to the porcelain tray.

I am a sandcastle girl, Jennifer thought, and ****** is the tide. Soon there will be nothing left.

The sight faded in one of her eyes and with the other she watched the last particles of her being circle away down the drain.

Venetian Gothic

CARMINE DIABLO

It was the sort of bar where you might intend to stop for one drink, but end up staying far too long. A place where the bartender asked no questions; somewhere that you might later recall, but with nothing approaching a solid memory. It was in an alleyway ten minutes' walk from Venice's *Santa Lucia* station, between a shop selling carnival masks to tourists and another providing plumbing supplies to locals, and when Jake found it open at seven in the morning he offered up a silent prayer that at least one thing in his life wasn't going to total shit.

He pushed the door and walked inside. As his eyes adjusted to the gloom he saw it was empty, just a barman staring at his phone. Jake approached; the guy didn't look up. He picked up the menu and turned it over and back, and then coughed. He tried to remember how to ask for a beer and a large vodka, before launching hesitantly into '*Buongiorno, posso…*' – right as the barman looked up and cut him off.

'You want a beer?'

How did they always *know* he was English?

Handsome and unshaven in a *Don't Worry Be Happy* t-shirt, the barman filled a glass with equal quantities of Moretti and foam and pushed it across. He stared at Jake for a moment.

'You want something else?' he asked.

'Vodka. Double,' Jake said. 'Please.'

The barman took a bottle of Stolichnaya Black Label from the shelf and filled a tumbler to the rim.

'*Grazie*,' Jake replied, nodding.

'*Prego*.'

He took out his wallet but the barman waved his hand.

'You pay later,' he said, turning away.

Jake sat down at a table in the corner, took a sip of vodka and pulled out his phone. The screen sprung to life, and there she was – Serena, draped over him, eyes alight, a smile like mischief. He threw back the rest of his drink remembering taking this on the night before they'd set off; a summer ahead travelling the beaches, galleries, bars and cheap hotels of Europe. They'd planned to do it all. Here in Venice they were going to see the paintings at the *Scuola Grande di San Rocco*, drink Bellinis at Harry's Bar, and marvel at the beauty of the Doge's Palace. It was to be a holiday that would bind them together, with memories to last a lifetime. Tales to tell the grandchildren. Sure, it was a cliché, but he'd never felt this way about anyone. And then five days in, Serena had dumped him. In Paris. Fucking Paris, city of romance. What total fucking bullshit.

'What total fucking bullshit,' bellowed a voice from across the room.

Jake looked up, startled. It was then he saw that the bar was not empty after all, and that sitting at another table were three elderly men.

The speaker was American, generously bearded, and with a face that managed to seem both kindly and pugnacious. He looked like a favourite uncle who would tousle your hair affectionately with one hand before punching you in the balls with the other. He sat opposite a much older man whose tatty-looking clothes, hair and skin were different shades of grey. His hands were restless, as jittery as rats on a leash. The two of them were ignoring a third man who was smaller, primly dressed and bookish, and whose gaze was fixed on the older fellow. He was less imposing, yet Jake couldn't help feeling there was a disturbing quality to him. It was the way he stared, with the eyes of an unsuccessful pervert.

The bearded man turned his attention to the large wine

glass filled with water in front of him, shaking his head at it, and murmuring sorrowfully, 'Every single time.'

'Why do you never learn, *compagno*?' the grey man replied in a rich Italian brogue.

'Who asked you, fuck-knuckle?' the bearded American snapped.

'How dare you speak to *il maestro* like that?' The smaller man said with passion, sitting bolt upright. 'Have you no respect? Why, this man –'

'Yeah, yeah, the greatest artist who ever lived, *blah blah blah*. Give it a rest will you, JR, I've heard it a thousand times.'

'And you'll hear it again, Papa, until you admit you're in the presence of genius.'

'Genius my ass! He painted pictures.'

'A worthier venture than making up stories, I suggest. That would seem to be the preserve of children, wouldn't you say?' the smaller man sneered.

'Siding with this decrepit ball-sack as always,' the American replied. 'What the hell did I do to deserve getting stuck here with you two shit-heels?' He threw his hands up to the heavens. 'What?'

'*Silenzio*. Gentlemen, please!' the grey man exclaimed. 'What time is it?' He swivelled his head from side to side as though looking for a clock. Jake's eavesdropping was interrupted when without warning, all three men turned towards him.

'Hey, kid,' the American called, across the bar.

Jake touched an index finger to his chest.

'Yeah, you. Get over here.' He pulled out an empty chair and patted it. Then to the barman he shouted 'Al, bring us more drinks, *pronto*.'

Jake rose and walked to their table. The moment he sat down with them he was hit by an unpleasant smell, somewhere between stagnant canal water, damp earth and bonfire smoke; it made him think of descending the steps into a cellar.

'What's with the hard liquor at this time of day?' the American asked, nodding at the glass in Jake's hand, which to his surprise now appeared to be full again.

'Er… it's a long story… sorry, did you want me for something?' Jake replied, looking from one to the next.

'Come on, kid, spill the beans,' the American said, swiping a monstrous glass of red from a tray the barman appeared with.

The smaller man took a glass of water, and when a beer was offered to the grey man, he waved it away, muttering, 'I'm not staying.'

Jake took a tumblerful of vodka.

The American had fallen silent, staring at his wine with a look of such intense desire that Jake felt embarrassed to watch. And then, as the American slowly raised the glass to his lips, Jake saw the colour change from red to pink to the unmistakable hue of plain water. Slowly, the American placed the glass back on the table. He closed his eyes.

'Just once,' he uttered mournfully, under his breath.

'So,' the ancient grey Italian said softly, 'Tell us what brings you to this place?'

'I split up with my girlfriend. Last night. In Paris.' Jake surprised himself at revealing his private misery to these three old goats. He was also surprised that hearing himself say it out loud seemed to lessen the pain, just a fraction.

'A blessing,' the bookish man said. 'We do not

need women to fulfil us, am I not right, Jacopo?'

The older man shrugged, non-committal.

'Do *not* listen to this creepy little fuck,' the American replied. 'Does he strike you as someone to ask for advice about women? Women are like trolley cars, kid, there's always another one coming down the track so stop moping. Get out there and move onto the next. Swear to God if I wasn't stuck in this stinking hole, I'd be right behind you.'

'You are both wrong, of course. A woman can offer salvation and she can deliver despair. In the end it does not matter. The work is all that matters. Only the work.' As the oldest man spoke, Jake noticed that he appeared to glow, his grey aura changing to a deep, shimmering crimson. At the same moment as this trick of the light, Jake heard the smaller man emit what sounded like the tiniest moan of pleasure, but then once each had dispensed their advice, such as it was, the men appeared to slip into silent contemplation. As they did, Jake noticed the strange, swampy smell begin to fade.

After several awkward moments, he slunk back to his table, sipped at his drinks and thought about Serena. When he checked the time he was astonished to see eight hours had passed, and Jake saw that what little light there'd been in the bar had gone, the darkness folding itself around him. He went to stand up, but it was as though a heavy weight was pressing him down. Three times he rose and three times he slumped back in his seat. At last, with an immense effort, he managed to stand.

'*Il conto, per favore*,' he said, approaching the bar. 'Can I pay for their drinks too? Those guys seem like they could do with a break.'

'No charge,' the barman replied, barely looking up from his phone.

‘They already paid?’ Jake turned to their table, but it was empty.

The barman locked eyes with him. At that moment the bell of a clock-tower chimed somewhere outside. ‘You are my only customer today,’ he replied.

‘But you brought ... the American had the wine that ... ’ Jake wasn’t sure how to finish.

The barman smiled, an expression that while appearing to contain all the right elements, managed to convey a surprising level of menace, and clearly invited no further discussion.

‘Would you like to stay for another drink?’ the barman asked. ‘It’s on the house.’

‘I should probably go,’ Jake replied with unexpected conviction.

‘Yes. I think that is for the best,’ the barman said, turning back to his phone.

Concrete

ANNIE FRIEDLEIN

Laila tries Mark's phone for the fourth time, but he doesn't answer. She glances at the clock and finds it's nine p.m., late enough to be angry. If she doesn't get his readings it means a late start for her demolition, and it's still possible the two of them could get black-listed, even after all this time. She fills her glass and drains it before capping the bottle. It's not like him. He's reliable, as assistants go. Perhaps his wife's not well? He'd asked to do extra hours, to save up for their baby, and Laila gave him the chance to work her own shifts, partly to be nice, but also to allow time with Kai, who's being difficult.

Either way, she's going to have to go to the radar station and find out what's going on. Through the window she can see the easterly edge of the city as it bleeds into the marshes. That's where Mark is supposed to be, working in the bunker and watchtower. She puts away the wine, staring out to sea after she shuts the fridge door. Patrol boats crawl across the estuary, their search lights dipping on a swell. It's a rough night, wind teasing the water. The moon stares back at her, mouth open.

'Kai, love,' she says, walking over to the table, 'I'm going to have to go out. A site visit.'

He looks up, work-screen lighting a strip of stubble on his jaw. 'So you can't listen to my talk then.'

'Yes, of course, I won't be long. It's a big job, the radar place, and I – '

'Yeah. Right. They're always big.'

She drags on her waterproofs and checks her sensor is in the pocket. 'No-one will expect the presentation to be perfect, don't worry.'

'Tell yourself that, Mum.'

Laila tucks her hair under a hat that Timmo bought her,

and it brings her up short for a second or so, remembering unwrapping that lying in bed on her birthday, with Kai still a baby, resting on a pillow between them. 'I know it's hard, reading the history of it,' she says to him. 'The enquiry said the sentry fired warning shots, but the Marsh people kept coming. It was a military site – those people could have been anyone.'

'Oh, sure. The Russians often send kids in as an invasion force.'

'Don't talk like that,' she says. The local teachers get worked up around the flood anniversaries, hyping the students. But Kai can't be heard saying this kind of thing. 'Write what you've been told to. Keep to the *facts*.'

'I would, if we knew what they were.' He shrugs and goes back to his presentation. He looks more and more like Timmo, with his wide chest draped in a baggy t-shirt, and long legs in stripey-socked feet.

She stops at the door. 'Be careful, please. Don't –.'

'What. Take risks? I'm not the one going out in the dark.'

Laila goes down, her reflection tense in the stairwell mirror, and gets in her car. It sets off automatically when she dictates the address and takes her along a wide street that was once flanked with terraced houses but now home to tower blocks with everyone living and gardening above fifteen metres in case the waters come back. She is driven past rows of warehouses and retail units that are due for dismantling, boxy places she ate in as a teen with other kids from the children's home. In a few years there will be nothing much left of that era, not here, anyway. She doesn't care. She's got Kai. There's nothing wrong with renewal.

She was away at a conference when it happened, missing the great surge of tidal water and the deaths of a family of

Marsh dwellers when a sniper killed them as they sought sanctuary. Seven people, some children, on the site where she and Mark are working. Opinion was fiery against the government at first, but that changed when the Ministry created a new strategy for Anglia, offering well-paid jobs to permanent locals. Laila never felt bad about signing up, as work had been in short supply before. Now, it's as if the Marsh folk never existed, and that's not a bad thing. There were a few who survived, and they went inland, to the Fens. They had never integrated with normal residents anyway.

They reach the sentry point that marks the radar station boundary, and she lifts her badge to the camera to be driven deeper through the woods. She tries Mark's phone but gets his voicemail again.

After a minute they arrive at the foundations of the decommissioned Mess, the first part of the site she dismantled, her drones powdering the blocks and flying the concrete dust to the docks, where the Ministry ships it to sell to those in drier climes. She gets out. Her car has parked beside Mark's motorbike but there's no sign of him. The moon is high, and the few town lights cast a halo over the treetops. There's no-one patrolling; no-one in sight, only the squat hexagonal bunker and watchtower on the grass between the Mess and the reed-beds, and the sweep of the estuary beyond, the dark sea water capped with white. The marshes sprawl north. An arrow of geese speeds by, low off the water.

When she flicks the switches at the top of the steps only one floodlight comes on, leaving most of the site in shadow. A deer runs from the bunker into the rushes as it is exposed to sight. In front of her, Mark's boots have left imprints in the mud, and she follows them down an incline to the bunker. Its rusted door is open, though there's no reason to worry about that. Nothing to take if you don't have the drones to demolish the materials.

'Mark?'

The interior is empty, and though he hasn't sent the data he's obviously been here and prepared the walls, because the blocks are clean. But she needs the sensor readings to be sure. If he's missed as much as a strand of wire-wool, the drones will shut down as a precaution. You can only sell pure materials these days.

Laila crosses to the observation window that faces the Marsh, picking up pieces of glass. As far as she remembers, they'd agreed to leave this pane in, because glass melts under the lasers, unlike anything else. So why are there shards on the sill? She wishes she could ask Mark. She suddenly has questions, a host of them, but they are pushed aside by nerves. Every noise is ten times louder than during the day. The rustling in the rushes is like the crackling of a bonfire. The whine of a mosquito by her ear is like a precision drill. Her heart feels as if it might burst.

Well, she can get the readings and go home. She switches on her sensor, and it reads clear on the first wall, and the second, and then the third. A duck rockets up, so she stops to see. The water it flew up from is glossy in the arc lights, grisly with clumps of weeds. Is the sea washing closer? On the fifth wall, the sensor screen starts to flicker. Laila raises it to her face and finds it blank, but the image comes back, the line peaking and troughing to show the presence of a material other than concrete. Duh *du*, it reads, duh *du*. As she's trying to work out what's causing it, there's a movement on the grass, and she glances up.

'God, Mark,' she says, 'where have you been?'

But it's not Mark, it's a boy of about fourteen or fifteen, standing between Laila and the marshes. He has a mark on his forehead, and his skin is the colour of a wintry dawn sky.

Duh *du*, reads the sensor, in her hand, duh *du*. The line is distorting to the edges of the screen and the alarm is louder than she's ever heard it. She snaps it off, her hand shaking.

The boy has vanished. Laila can't move for a moment. It was a mistake to come here. She shouts through the broken window.

'You're trespassing. This is government property!'

No reply. The marshland lies bleached in now-flickering lights. She can't run for the car, it's too far to be sure she'll get there, and she'll be exposed all the way. Did Mark chase this wanderer away, or try to, and fall foul of him?

She waits. She breathes. After a while, when nothing stirs, a little reason returns. She thinks of her reputation, which is for common sense. The stray was a child, he's not going to hurt her. A patrol boat can't be far away, either. She turns the sensor back on to read the wall that is nearest to the watchtower. One more, and then she can go.

A fierce sound fills the bunker, the alarm so loud she drops the handset.

The boy has come inside the door. He has a curious gait as he walks towards her, moving too evenly over the ground. She steps back and starts to weep. He smells sharp and sour, of eel skin and salt-water. He is too close. She shuts her eyes and stops breathing, reaches out to shove him away. But there is nothing to press against.

'Please. I have a son,' she says, her voice sticking in her throat.

His smell becomes as thick as smoke. With her eyes half-shut she gropes for the window, trying to pull herself out through the frame, but she gets caught on the shards, gasping as they cut her palms. Her waterproofs tear as she struggles and drops through, to the ground. She crawls forward, and in the corner of her eye she can see feet and legs, indistinct, other presences keeping pace with her, and that smell is everywhere, despite the wind and the air. Her palms leave red streaks on the grass as she pulls herself forward. Her mind turns too slowly. Where can she go? The water is inviting her closer, and it feels like a haven, waves rolling faster through the reeds.

Kai, she thinks in desperation, though her son seems like a distant thing that might not even be real. She wills herself to believe she will get away. But if she doesn't, will the Ministry allow him to go to London and find Timmo? No, she thinks, but he will go there anyway.

There is a crackling of gunshot from the watchtower, and she does not need to turn to know that there is nobody there. She is in the fringes of the water, drawn to it against reason. It fills her mouth and ears as she drags herself forward, crawling, sinking. There is a large branch in front of her, a chance of a weapon, but when she snatches at it, it yields to her touch. A bearded face rolls over towards her in a mask of terror, and she sees Mark.

Laila is clutched and spun by an incoming wave. Mark's body washes over her in a tangle of deadweight. The boy is close to her, and when she twists onto her back, he is dark as a storm-cloud, and the other figures are fading. *I'm sorry*, she wants to cry out, but then why say that, when she isn't sorry at all? She's made choices, based on facts. They were good choices. The marsh claims her body as the sea washes in. Fronds coil and pierce and grip. As the arc light fails, a shot rings out. The boy forms a cross, arms outflung, like those on the old altars. Suspended for an instant between Laila and the moon, he carries her down, heavy as concrete.

Where It Hurt the Most

AMELIA BUTTERLY

Opening her mouth, Mae rested the soft flesh of Sennin's arm on her bottom incisors, then brought her upper jaw down. She clenched, inching her teeth closer together, feeling his skin shift against their edges.

Sometimes the need would become overwhelming. All she could think about was this, the feel of a cheek or a calf yielding to her bite. It was the creases that got her. Thick lines around wrist and elbow, ankle and knee. Once she had taken it too far, leaving faint indentations which she tried to rub away. Now Mae was more careful.

She relaxed her jaw and let Sennin's arm drop gently. He stirred against her and she tipped him up over her shoulder, letting him nestle into her neck while she rested her cheek on his skull. Outside a car door slammed and laughter bubbled through the cracked window. Mae flinched, pulling Sennin closer and twisting her body away from the sound. When a siren had passed by last night, it had taken hours to soothe him back to sleep, and her eyes had been heavy and sore all day.

For once she was lucky, and tonight he didn't stir. Mae breathed in, letting her muscles unwind a fraction. But they tightened again. She inhaled once, twice, sharp little snatches of air.

Sennin didn't smell like himself. He didn't smell of anything. She pushed her nose against his scalp, sniffing her way across the skin. Nothing. A complete absence of scent.

Mae patted her palm across the hillocks of duvet, trying to keep the rest of her body still. When she found her phone, she unlocked it one-handed, careful to tilt the glare away from the baby. This time though, it seemed the blue light didn't bother him. She thought about texting Alex but she didn't know what to say. He'd think she was being ridiculous, again. Awkwardly, the phone precarious, she opened a new tab and keyed in her question.

The usual websites popped up. A couple of pseudo-medical pages dedicated to the kinds of late-night searching done by new mothers everywhere. Some web forums where nicer people would respond "you got this mama" regardless of the issue. Lists of similar queries other people had posed. But nothing that answered the question, "Where has my baby's smell gone?"

Mae tried a couple of other search terms, deleting and retyping, her frustration growing. She clicked on "How often should you bathe a newborn?" and "At what age do babies develop a sense of smell?" But it was all useless.

Only when she tossed her phone on the bed with a soft thump, did she realise Sennin had slept through the brightening light on the screen and her restless, irritated wriggling. For weeks now, night after night she had sat rigid, bones and muscles locking in place. The slightest movement would wake him and she would have to begin the dreadful process of rocking and shushing and pacing all over again.

Mae peered down at him. Had she cracked it? Was he finally the kind of baby who knew how to sleep? A tiny mote of dust rested on his cheek and she caressed her thumb across it, challenging her touch to wake him. It didn't. But neither did it brush the dust away. Mae bent closer, trying to establish what had made the mark. She scratched a nail, expecting the bump of a scab, but it was smooth, as if the mark had been there all along. Maybe it had been there all along? But Mae knew every inch of his body - the birthmark on his foot, the light blue of his eyes - as well as her own.

She clawed back her phone, ready to ask it whether freckles could suddenly appear on a baby. As she stretched, the device shifted away from her grasp and slid to the laminate floor with a smack. Sennin barely moved. Unwilling to test the miracle any further, Mae inched back on the bed until her spine was propped up on the pillows, then pulled one of his balled-up hands toward her face. She uncurled his forefinger, and gently put it in her mouth, closing her eyes and feeling the thread of bone against her teeth.

Mae rolled over in bed, letting the heaviness in her legs help her deepen the stretch as she woke. It was still quiet out, and the room beyond her closed eyes felt dark and still.

Sennin!

Mae ripped the duvet from her body. Sennin wasn't underneath. She flung the pillows out her way, seeing his lifeless body wherever she looked. But the bed was empty. She scrabbled for the lamp, dusty with disuse. The glare made her blink as she scanned the floor, expecting to see him motionless, trauma to the head, blood pooling.

Instead, from the furthest corner, came a gurgling, a singsong noise she hadn't heard before. A foot emerged from a pile of dirty washing and waved about in the air.

The adrenalin ebbed as Mae struggled to stand, nausea roiling. Sleeping that deeply had made her feel worse than the nights where she hadn't closed her eyes. Mae tripped towards the mound of laundry as a second foot pushed its way out and began to flail. She hesitated, unsure why she was unwilling to bend down and pull back the top of the bundle.

She watched her hand reach out and take hold of the fabric, lifting it slowly. Another gurgle, almost a laugh this time. Mae bent down closer.

A tiny fist shot out, knocking against her shin and Mae stepped back with a shriek, her foot crunching down awkwardly on something that dug into the soft sole. She let out a little cry and bit it back, steadying herself.

She'd stood on a cheap plastic toy Alex's mum had bought, now in shards. Mae could have sworn she'd told Alex it was a choking hazard and stuffed it to the back of the wardrobe. Stop being ridiculous, she told herself, kicking the larger bits of plastic out of the way.

She picked up Sennin, holding him so he faced out. It wasn't how she normally carried him, but just at this moment, it felt right to keep him from looking at her. She walked into the living room and stood, letting her gaze run over the shadowy corners.

Sennin didn't seem phased by the new way he was being held, his back hot against Mae's chest. He carried on making the same lilting sounds, swinging his limbs rhythmically.

Fresh air. Her own mother's voice echoed from a distance into Mae's thoughts. Fresh air always clears the head. She wrenched open the metal door to the balcony, hinges squeaking, and stepped out onto the narrow concrete platform. The traffic was louder out here. Mae dragged in a deep breath, the tang of exhaust filling her nostrils. Her heartbeat seemed to be steadying. The air was chill, the last days of summer had bled away weeks ago. The flats opposite stretched up, pockmarked with glowing windows. Mae took a step forward, resting the baby's weight on the balcony rails and craned her neck towards the top of the block. Then she peered down to the ground, four floors below, trying to make out the patchwork of paving slabs and dirt.

"Sennin!"

He had swung his legs hard, the movement catching Mae off guard. She snatched him tight against her stomach, her fingers digging into his flesh. With her free hand she scrabbled for the door and backed through it, slamming it and turning the key before letting out a breath. Mae sank to the sofa and tears sprung to her eyes.

He squirmed in her lap, twisting his body to look at her. His fingertips scrabbled at her skin, pinching where it hurt the most, making her stomach turn. She finally let him face her. Their gaze met, Sennin's eyes dark and unfamiliar, and her insides lurched again. Mae dumped him on the rug at her feet and fled to the bedroom.

Her phone was still face down on the laminate. She dialled, but there was no answer.

"Alex," she typed, her fingers hard on the screen. "I need you."

She was typing another message when the reply came through.

"Is everything OK? You rang? I was asleep."

"It's Sennin. He's not right."

She rang again, but still Alex didn't answer.

"Are you still there? There's something really wrong with him."

"Temperature? Rash?"

"You're not getting it." Mae typed, deleted and then

retyped the next bit of the message. “I don’t think he’s Sennin anymore.”

This time the reply was quick. “Stay there. Don’t move. Don’t do anything. I’m coming.”

When Mae woke again, the weak autumn sun was fingering at the curtains. Her neck ached where she had been bent over, cradling Sennin in her arms. She opened her eyes and looked down at him, wide awake but motionless. The mark on his face was bigger, more permanent.

Her phone screen lit up with a warning that her battery was about to give up. It was later than she first thought. Surely Alex should have come back by now?

Mae scrolled to her messages, clicked on Alex’s name. She thumbed the screen up and down. There was nothing there, no messages from the night before. She clicked in and out again, looking for updates. Nothing. Her skin prickled and nausea budded in her throat.

In her arms, Sennin stretched, his back arching. He let out a yawn.

No-one is coming. No-one knows.

He started singing, that same noise he had been making, but louder than ever. Mae stumbled to her feet and left the bedroom. She reached the balcony and turned the key in the lock. The cool autumn air tumbled into the room, and she stepped outside.

Authors

Jamie Bolt has worked as a journalist, librarian and creative writing tutor, and recently completed his first novel. He studied at King's College, London, and the British Institute in Paris.

Amelia Butterly is an award-winning journalist and writer working on her first novel. She lives in south London with her son.

Laura Cooper is a writer, photographer and educator based in Norwich, Norfolk. She writes short stories about strange events and is exploring the idea of *solastalgia* through a climate-fiction novel.

Carmine Diablo is a psychology teacher, sight-running tour guide and fourth-level stone balancer. His stories have been performed at the Liars' League and commended in the Yeovil Literary Prize. He writes for the *Times Educational Supplement*.

Annie Friedlein, Larder Collective founder, lives in Hertfordshire. She has MA degrees from the Universities of Cambridge, London, and East Anglia.

Nicole Hazan is a fiction writer from England and Israel. She has an MA in Creative Writing from UEA. She lives with her husband and twin daughters in Tel Aviv and is working on a psychological thriller.

Rob Passmore lives in East London and works in housing regeneration. He has written film scripts, magazine articles, short stories and a novel that is forever on the verge of completion.

Simon Wroe, editor of *Disturbance*, is an author, freelance journalist, teacher and former chef whose first novel *Chop Chop* won a Betty Trask award and was listed for the Costa Prize, while *Here Comes Trouble* was listed for the Bollinger Everyman.

Acknowledgements

Thank you to Simon Wroe for editing the stories, to Jamie Bolt and Jennifer Cameron for proofing them, to Sarah Whittaker for her cover design, to Andrew Chapman for his guidance, to Ashley Friedlein for his generosity, and to all the writers of the Larder Collective for another inspiring collaboration.

Printed in Great Britain
by Amazon

17497738R00048